Pitschi

The Kitten Who Always Wanted to Be Something Else:
A Sad Story that Ends Well

by Hans Fischer

Translated by Marianne Martens

NorthSouth
New York / London

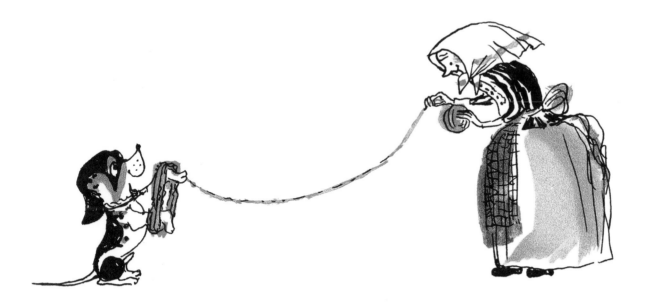

Old Lisette was sitting in front of her house knitting, surrounded by her pets. Sleeping on the bench next to her were the cats Mauli and Ruli. Their five kittens had just turned six weeks old. Two of them, Grigri and Groggi, were wrestling. Patschi was playing with a ball of wool, and Negri was trying to climb the broom. But the last one, the smallest and daintiest of them all, wasn't playing like the others. She just sat in the basket, dreaming. Her name was Pitschi. Good old Bello the dog watched her thoughtfully. He was very worried about this kitten that didn't play like the others.

When Lisette went into the kitchen, Bello ran after her. Mauli and Ruli slept on peacefully, but Grigri, Groggi, Patschi, and Negri started to misbehave. They grabbed Lisette's knitting, playing with it until it was all unraveled. Then they knocked over the broom and happily climbed up on it. Pitschi was not amused. She left the yard and went looking for something else entirely.

Behind the house were Lisette's chickens. When Pitschi saw the cute little chicks, she wanted to play with them, but the mother hen absolutely would not allow it. She called all her children together and hurried off with them. Father rooster came to the rescue; but when he saw that it was just a little kitten that mother hen was running from, he turned around and proudly strutted away.

"I want to be a proud rooster like that," thought Pitschi, strutting after him. She managed to walk after the rooster on two legs and scratched for seeds in the dirt just like him. She even crowed—almost as well as the big rooster—and soon they were competing to see who could crow the loudest.

Their crowing annoyed the rooster next door, and soon there was a cockfight.

"Oh, no!" cried Pitschi. "I don't want to be a rooster after all!" She ran off into the fields, where she found a large but kind-looking animal, Lisette's goat.

"I want to be a goat," said Pitschi. So the kindly goat gave Pitschi a bell to wear. Pitschi put two branches on her head to make horns. "Do I look like you?" she asked the goat. "Yes, exactly!" the goat replied. But just then Lisette came to milk the goat.

"Oh, no!" cried Pitschi. "I don't want to be a goat after all!" And disappointed,
she ran away.

Pitschi soon met someone new, a duck who was busy grooming herself. "I can do that just as well as you can," said Pitschi, and she began to lick herself. "I want to be a duck," Pitschi decided, and she waddled off to the pond. The ducks slipped into the water one at a time and swam away. It looked easy, so Pitschi tried it too.

Oh, no! Pitschi sank, and would have drowned if she hadn't been saved by a clever duck who dived under and reemerged with Pitschi sitting on her back. The duck carried Pitschi safely to the shore, where mother rabbit and her babies watched, astonished.

They waited until she was not quite so wet, and then the bunnies got braver, sniffing Pitschi's whiskers with their warm noses. Pitschi just sat there happily. "I want to be a bunny," she thought.

As the ducks left, the little bunnies timidly approached Pitschi. They didn't get too close at first, because she was dripping wet.

When evening came, mother rabbit called to her children: "Hurry home, it's bedtime."
The bunnies were obedient and didn't make their mother call them twice. And since Pitschi
had decided to be a bunny too, she hopped along to the hutch with them.

When it was dark, Lisette closed all the cages so her animals would be safe. She didn't know that Pitschi was in the rabbit hutch. The kitten, still shivering from her swim in the pond, had curled up among the bunnies for warmth. She was so tired that she fell asleep immediately.

In the middle of the night, Pitschi woke up. She had no idea where she was, but she knew that she wanted to go back home to Lisette. She started to cry: "Miao, miao!"

The moon had risen, and Pitschi saw dark animals coming out of the woods toward the hutch. They came closer and closer—all the way to the bars! The fox opened its big mouth, and the owl stared with its scary eyes. Pitschi was terribly afraid, and cried louder and louder. Didn't anyone hear her?

Bello heard. He barked until Lisette woke up. She turned on the light and opened
the window. Bello leaped out of the window and chased the fox and the owl away.
Then he searched for Pitschi; and with his good sense of smell, he found her quickly.
She wasn't crying anymore, but she was frozen from fear.

Lisette carried Pitschi home.

She dried her and wrapped her up warmly.

Then she gave her milk from a bottle.

The next morning Pitschi was very ill. All the animals came to visit, and it was easy to see

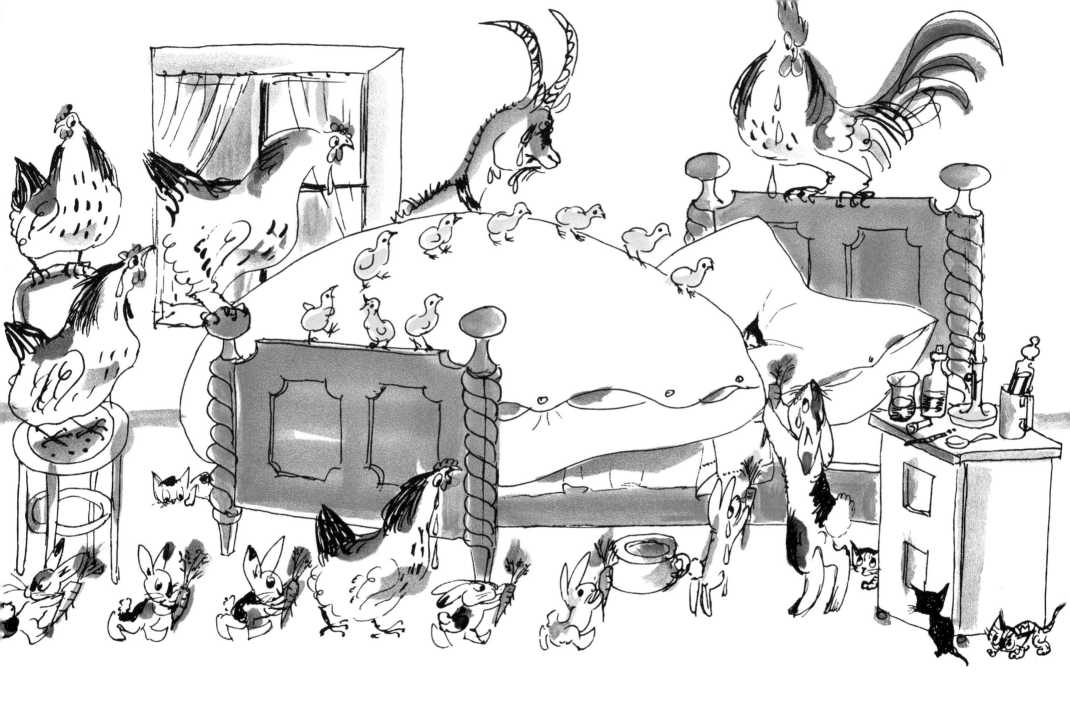

they were all very fond of her. The kittens weren't playing anymore. Everyone was sad.

Day after day Pitschi got better, but she was still very weak. Then Bello had a good idea.
He built a little wagon out of the kittens' basket. Father Mauli brought Lisette's parasol as
a roof for the wagon, and mother Ruli brought a soft pillow.

Pitschi was glad to finally be allowed to go outside again. But she still couldn't forget that horrible night. All the animals wanted to cheer her up, so they planned something fun—a big party in Lisette's flower garden. Mauli, Ruli, and Bello brought Pitschi over in the wagon.

The party was great fun. The last ones to stop playing and dancing were the kittens—including Pitschi. How she loved playing cat and mouse!

When the other animals had gone, Lisette called to the family of cats, "Get cleaned up and come to the table—I've prepared a treat."

Bello brought in the surprise—a gigantic cake covered in whipped cream. Pitschi sat with a pillow behind her back because she was still recovering. She looked at Lisette and thought, "What a nice lady." And from then on, Pitschi didn't want to be anything but a kitten, safe at home with Lisette, sitting at the cat table.

Copyright © 1993 by NordSüd Verlag AG, CH-8005 Zürich, Switzerland.
First published in Switzerland in 1947 by Artemis Verlag, Zuirch, under the title *Pitschi*.
First published in the United States by Harcourt, Brace & Company, Inc., 1953.
English translation copyright © 1996 by North-South Books Inc., New York 10001.
Reissued in 2010 by North-South Books Inc., New York 10001.
All rights reserved.
No part of this book may be reproduced or utilized in any form or by any means, electronic or mechanical,
including photo-copying, recording, or any information storage and retrieval system, without permission
in writing from the publisher.
Distributed in the United States by North-South Books Inc., New York 10001.

Library of Congress Cataloging-in-Publication Data is available.
A CIP catalogue record for this book is available from The British Library.
ISBN: 978-0-7358-2278-8 (trade edition)
Printed in China by Toppan Leefung Packaging & Printing (Dongguan) Co., Ltd.,
Dongguan, P.R.C., December 2009.
1 3 5 7 9 ⊶ 10 8 6 4 2
www.northsouth.com

Hans Fischer

fis

1909–1958

HANS FISCHER, who was known by his trademark signature, *fis*, was one of the most popular Swiss children's book illustrators in the years following World War II and an important influence in the field of children's book illustration throughout the world.

Born in Bern, he attended the School of Fine Arts and Industrial Arts in Geneva, and the School of Art and Commerce in Zurich. He worked as an advertising artist, a window decorator, a filmmaker, and a stage designer and set painter for the legendary Cabaret Cornichon in Zurich. He was also well known as a muralist, and his bright, childlike works still decorate the walls of schools in Switzerland.

Among the fairy tales he illustrated for children were picture book versions of "The Bremen Town Musicians" and an adaptation of "Puss in Boots." He also wrote and illustrated two picture books, *The Birthday Party* and *Pitschi*, both featuring kind old Lisette and her animals. They were created as gifts for Fischer's own children, who used to watch him work and begged for stories featuring all the things they loved best. Both of these books, but *Pitschi* in particular, demonstrate Fischer's fondness for cats, which played a large role in all of his work. Surrounded by cats in his studio, he studied their movements and made hundreds of sketches of them.

Pitschi is also a perfect example of the artist's mastery of stone lithography, a printmaking process more commonly used for fine art than for illustration. To create the book, Fischer drew the pictures directly on large stones—one for each color.

More importantly, *Pitschi* and its companion volume, *The Birthday Party*, epitomize the insouciant charm and singular artistry that characterize Hans Fischer's work. "As children's books these two volumes are perhaps the ones to be most treasured," wrote Betinna Hurlimann in *Three Centuries of Children's Books in Europe*, "for they contain everything to delight young people. They are full of the wit and kindliness, the color and happiness, the great good humor of a man who turned into a child again among his own children."